A Giant First-Start Reader

This easy reader contains only 40 different words, repeated often to help the young reader develop word recognition and interest in reading.

Basic word list for *First Day of Spring*

a	do	special
and	feel	Spring
animals	feels	sun
are	first	sweet
baby	flowers	the
because	fresh	they
birds	hear	things
bright	is	today
busy	it	very
can	know	warm
children	of	what
chirping	playing	with
day	see	you
	smell	

First Day of Spring

Written by Sharon Gordon

Illustrated by Christine Willis

Troll Associates

Library of Congress Cataloging in Publication Data

Gordon, Sharon.
    First day of spring.

    Summary: Describes special feelings, smells,
sounds, and sights of the first day of spring.
    [1. Spring—Fiction]   I. Willis, Christine.
II. Title.
PZ7.G65936Fi   [E]   81-2750
ISBN 0-89375-531-1   AACR2
ISBN 0-89375-532-X (pbk.)

Today is a very special day.

Do you know what day it is?

Today, you can *feel* special things.

The sun feels special today.

It is bright and warm.

You can feel the warm sun.

Today, you can *smell* special things.

The flowers smell special today.

They smell sweet and fresh.

You can smell the sweet flowers.

Today, you can *hear* special things.

You can hear the busy birds today.
The busy birds are chirping.

You can hear the birds chirping.

Today, you can *see* special things.

You can see baby animals today.

The baby animals are playing.

You can see the baby animals playing.

Today, you can see the children playing.

They feel the warm sun.

They smell the sweet flowers.

They hear the birds chirping.

They see the baby animals playing.

The children are playing with the baby animals.

Today is a very special day.

You can feel, and smell, and hear and
see special things.

Because today is the first day of Spring!